MAMA

This book belongs to

_____

Oh, how I long to be held
in your embrace,

To feel your soft skin
rubbing gently against my face.

Your sweet smell, your warm skin, and the sound of your heartbeat,

Always made me feel whole, safe, and complete.

Oh,
how I long to hear you

sing a lullaby,
That gently rocked me to sleep.

My eyes would close,
and I would smile,

As I was lulled into
a beautiful dream.

I dreamed of you holding me and telling me that everything was alright.

You told me you would always be around, and then you would squeeze me tight.

But ELOHIM had a better plan for you, Mama, because HE called you home.

HE assured me that HE left me a comforter and I would never be alone.

My heart misses you so much
and
wishes that you were still here.

To hold me in your warm embrace

and dry all my tears.

The memory of your loving smile

will always be in my heart,

As long as I know this,

we will never be apart.

Draw a picture of mom

Sabrina Kirkland
Author, CEO
My Name is M.E.

In 2005, Sabrina started working with victims of human trafficking. It is in this role that she found her passion. Chairing the subcommittee of the Florida Abolitionist, she worked closely with the Department of Children and Families (DCF), the Florida Department of Law Enforcement, the Department of Juvenile Justice, FBI, Metropolitan Bureau of Investigation, the National Center for Missing & Exploited Children (NCMEC), and the state and local law enforcement.

Sabrina has been certified to train trainers, teachers, and law enforcement and DCF workers about Domestic Minor Sex Trafficking (DMST) and how to recognize victims. In 2012, Sabrina started her company: My Name Is M.E. LLC, advocating for the eradication of human trafficking, sexual child abuse, teen domestic violence, and bullying. She is also the founder of Seed Life Foundation Inc., which is a nonprofit organization that will build life-skill centers for homeless youth.

Contact Us
800-295-4508
info@mynameis.me
4644 Powder Springs Road #892

Made in the USA
Middletown, DE
05 May 2022

65302218R00015